Wishbone ran from **place and headed for the door!**

"There you are!" boomed the custodian, stepping in front of him. "Come here, you!"

Wishbone turned. He crawled under a row of desks in the classroom. "I'm . . . uh . . . just a piece of chalk! Rolling along. No?"

The man continued to look for him. There was only one way out—

Wishbone ran between the man's legs!

"Stop! Stop, you!" said the custodian.

The teacher's desk! It had to be too big for the man to lift! Wishbone dived under the chair and slid beneath the desk. He scrunched into a corner. He hoped the man hadn't seen where he had gone—

"Oh, no! A hand!" Wishbone said. It was reaching ___ m. . . .

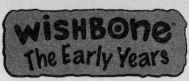

Jack
and the
Beanstalk

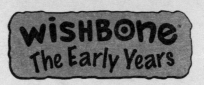

Wishbone
The Early Years

Jack and the Beanstalk

by Brad Strickland and Thomas E. Fuller
WISHBONE™ created by Rick Duffield

SCHOLASTIC INC.

New York Toronto London Auckland Sydney
Mexico City New Delhi Hong Kong

ISBN 0-439-12835-8

12 11 10 9 8 7 6 5 4 3 2   9/9 0 1 2 3 4/0

Printed in the U.S.A.   40

First Scholastic printing, September 1999

Edited by Kevin Ryan
Continuity editing by Grace Gantt
Copy edited by Cathy Dubowski
Cover design by Lyle Miller
Interior illustrations by Kathryn Yingling

For Dr. Samuel Smiley, friend and vet
—Brad Strickland

*This book is dedicated to my mother,
Anne Fuller, who always had time for stories—
and for her children. Thanks, Mom.*
—Thomas E. Fuller

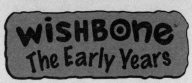

Jack and the Beanstalk

A WORD FROM OUR TOP DOG . . .

Helllooo! Wishbone here. Welcome to my brand-new series of books, **Wishbone: The Early Years**. These books tell the story of my adventures as a puppy, when my best friend, Joe, and his friends were eight years old and in third grade.

In this story I face a big, scary custodian who reminds me of the giant in the classic fairy tale **"Jack and the Beanstalk."** I imagine that I am Jack, who has a big adventure on a magical beanstalk. You're in for a real treat, so pull up a chair, grab a snack, and sink your teeth into *Jack and the Beanstalk!*

Chapter One

Lost Ball!

"Mom," Joe Talbot said, "I have to bring something to school for show-and-tell."

Joe's mom was Ellen Talbot. She smiled at her eight-year-old son. "What do you want to bring?" she asked.

Wishbone had been lying in his big red chair. He jumped up and wagged his tail. "I know! I know! Take the puppy!"

"I don't know," Joe said to his mom. "Miss Basso said it should be something special."

Wishbone jumped down from his chair. He ran over to Joe. "Puppies are special! Take me! Take the puppy!"

Ellen put on her thinking face. "You could take your softball bat. Or maybe your basketball."

Joe shrugged. "I guess I could. But I want to do something different. What could I take that would be something no one else would bring?"

Wishbone barked.

"I know!" Ellen said. "You could take Wishbone!"

Wishbone felt happy. "Yes! Yes! Take the puppy! I'd love to find out where you go all day, Joe! I want to know what school is like! Please take me!"

"That's a great idea," Joe said. "Thanks, Mom!"

Wishbone bowed. "Thank you, Ellen!"

Later, Wishbone thought he might need to bring something for show-and-tell, too. What could he take? His food dish? His water bowl? Then he thought of something very special. He would take his first squeaky toy. It

2

looked just like a small soccer ball. Wishbone got his soccer ball and dropped it inside his pet carrier. The carrier was a big plastic box with a door. He was ready to go.

That morning, Ellen drove Joe and Wishbone to school. Wishbone traveled inside his pet carrier. The puppy peeked through his pet door. He tried to poke his black nose through one of the grate openings and sniffed and sniffed.

When he arrived at Oakdale Elementary School, Wishbone smelled new scents as he neared the building. He could smell the green grass of the playground and the chalk from the chalkboards. Best of all, he smelled the lunchroom! Wishbone licked his chops. He could not wait for lunch! He was sure the school's food would be great!

Joe's classroom was bright and cheerful. Miss Basso, his teacher, was a pretty woman with blond hair. The moment she saw Wishbone, she said, "How cute!"

All the boys and girls in the room wanted to pet him. Wishbone came out of his pet carrier and played with them. He knew some of them. David Barnes was there. He was one of Joe's best friends. David lived next door to Joe and Wishbone. Samantha Kepler was there, too. She was Joe's other best friend. Everyone called her Sam. She scratched Wishbone's ears. Mmm! He liked that!

"Good boy," Sam said. "I hope you like being at school!"

When show-and-tell began, Wishbone saw that Joe was getting nervous. The boy kept clearing his throat, and he was breathing hard.

Wishbone hoped his friend would do well. He worried so much about Joe that he forgot to be nervous himself.

Finally, it was Joe's turn. He stood up and led Wishbone to the front of the class. Joe took a deep breath and began.

"This is my dog, Wishbone," Joe said. "Let me tell you how he got his name. It started when my family was having dinner one night. Dad and I pulled on a turkey wishbone, and I won. I wished for a puppy. Dad surprised me

and brought home a puppy the next day. I named him Wishbone!"

Joe's voice was a little shaky. Wishbone knew that sometimes Joe felt sad when he thought about his dad. Steve Talbot had died from a rare blood disease.

Wishbone felt happy as Joe continued his story. He told the boys and girls how he took care of Wishbone. "I have to watch out for him," Joe said. "He's still just a puppy. He might get into trouble if I don't take good care of him. But I like to care for him because he's my best friend."

Wishbone smiled. "Great job, Joe!" Joe returned to his desk. Wishbone walked by his side.

Wishbone enjoyed the rest of the school day. He played with Joe and his friends for a while. Then Joe took him outside for a quick walk. After that, he and Joe ate lunch in the school lunchroom.

Back in the classroom later, Wishbone

had to be quiet while Joe and his friends learned reading. Wishbone got his soccer ball out of his carrier. He went into a corner of the room and took a nap. Then he woke up and played with his ball. The reading lesson was over.

"Children," Miss Basso said, "let's line up for recess."

Recess! That meant going outside! Wishbone looked for a place to hide his soccer ball. He found a good spot and dropped his ball there. Then he ran outside to play!

He couldn't remember the last time he had had so much fun. Wishbone ran and jumped. He played tag with Joe's friends. He fetched sticks. By the end of recess he was one tired puppy. When everyone got back to the classroom, Wishbone crept into his carrier and took another nap.

He didn't wake up until school ended and Joe put the carrier into Ellen's car. Then Wishbone sat up quickly. "Hey! We can't leave yet!"

"Did you have a good day?" Ellen asked Joe.

Joe said, "I sure did! I think Wishbone did, too. He's really tired from playing."

Wishbone scratched at the carrier. "My ball! I left my ball! We have to go back!"

Ellen didn't seem to hear. She drove Joe and Wishbone home.

As soon as Wishbone was out of his carrier, he began to beg to go back to the school. "That's my favorite ball! I have to go back and get it! Please? Please, please, please?"

"I'll make dinner," Ellen said.

Wishbone flopped down on the floor. "No one ever listens to the puppy. Just wait until I'm a big dog! Then everyone will listen to me!"

He thought if he were big enough, he could simply go outside, run to the school, and get his ball back. *Too bad I'm still a puppy*, he thought.

Wishbone wanted his ball. Somehow, that reminded him of a story. "Hmm . . . something I need is missing. And it is a long way off, in a very big building. What does that make me think of? It is a great old story. Oh, I know! This is just like the fairy tale of 'Jack and the Beanstalk'!"

Even though Wishbone was only a little puppy, he had a big imagination. He began to think about the story of Jack. Then he started to imagine that he *was* Jack. Just like Wishbone, Jack had trouble. . . .

Chapter Two

The Deal of the Century

Hi, all! This is Wishbone! Did you know that children and puppies alike have been enjoying the story "Jack and the Beanstalk" for hundreds of years? It comes from England. Over the years many people told the story of Jack in a lot of ways. From time to time, the tale was also translated into several foreign languages. In fact, the version I'm going to tell is based on two books. One was written in London, England, in 1807. The other was written in Philadelphia in 1809. That is almost two hundred years ago!

Wishbone began to imagine he lived in England long ago. It was during the make-believe time of fairy tales. It was a time when brave knights fought dragons, and magic was everywhere. He imagined he was a poor boy named Jack Terrier, who lived with his mother. The small family was very poor.

Jack's mother was too sick to work. He had tried to find a job himself, but had failed. Everyone thought he was too young to work.

Jack came home one afternoon so tired he could hardly move. He had walked for miles trying to find work. Jack was hot and tired. Most of all, he was hungry. He had gone to bed hungry the night before, and he had been hungry that morning when he woke up.

His mother opened the door as he came to their poor little house. She was a thin, pale woman. "No luck?" she asked.

11

Jack's tail drooped as he walked into the kitchen. "No. No one wants to hire me because I'm too young. I tell everyone that I'm smart, but no one believes me." He sighed. "Mother, do we have anything for dinner?"

"There's only milk," his mother said sadly.

Disappointed, Jack climbed up on a chair and lay down. He wanted something more solid than milk. "We already had milk for breakfast," he said.

"I know, dear," Jack's mother said. She patted the fur on his head. "I'm sorry, but that's all we have."

Jack sat up on his hind legs and thought hard. "I think I see our problem. It shouldn't be just 'milk.' It should be 'milk *and* oatmeal,' or 'milk *and* eggs,' or even 'milk *and* bread.' Our trouble is that we don't have any 'and' to go with the milk!"

"All we own now is our cow, Blossom," said Jack's mother. "And she doesn't give oatmeal or eggs or bread. Just milk."

"I wish we had more," Jack said.

His mother looked so sad that a chill ran down the fur on his back.

"I'm sorry, Mom," Jack said. "I know you do your best. I know you're hungry, too."

"Yes, I am, Jack," said his mother. "I wish we had beautiful clothes and a nice place to live. In this old house, the roof leaks, the floor creaks, and the mice creep. When your father was alive, we lived in a very nice house."

13

Jack always felt sad when his mother talked about his dad. He had died so long ago that Jack could hardly remember him. Jack lay down on the floor and thought about his father. "What happened to Dad?" he asked.

"It was very, very sad," his mother told him. "Your father was a good man. He traveled all over the world. He had many adventures. He brought home some wonderful treasures."

Jack raised his head. Both of his pointed ears perked up. "Treasures?"

"Yes," his mother said. "He brought home a goose that laid golden eggs."

"Golden eggs! You can't beat them!" Jack said, excited by the story.

"What?" his mother asked.

"Well," Jack said, laughing, "they would bend your eggbeater."

Jack's mother smiled at his joke.

"What else did Dad have?" Jack asked.

"Oh," said his mother, "he had a wonderful

magic harp. All by itself, it could play any song you wanted. It filled the house with music."

Jack thought about that. "It would be nice to have music in the house. I wish we still had the harp. Did Dad have anything else?"

His mother thought. "He had a magic axe," she said. "It would chop wood all by itself. He would just point to a tree and say, 'Axe, axe, work for me! Chop, chop, chop! Chop down that tree!' We sold the wood and the golden eggs. We had enough money to buy a nice house and plenty of food."

"What happened to the treasures?" Jack asked. "Why don't we have the goose and the harp and the axe now?"

"Because a giant heard about them," his mother said. "No one knows where he came from. And no one knows where he went. But one day the giant came and took all your father's treasures. When your dad tried to stop him, the giant stepped on him. That is how your father died."

"That's awful!" Jack said.

The next day Jack searched for work again. All the farmers said, "You're too small to be much help." So they wouldn't hire him.

Jack knew he was smart and could learn to do anything, but he could not get the chance to try. He went home feeling so hungry he could hardly walk. That made him think of his dad, and his heart felt empty and sad.

When Jack got to his house, he asked his mom, "Don't we even have a little cheese?"

"No," his mother said. "We ate the cheese days ago."

"Don't we have some bread?" Jack asked, scratching his chin with his hind foot.

"No," his mother said. "We ate the bread with the cheese."

"Oh, I remember now," said Jack. "We had grilled-cheese sandwiches." His mouth watered when he thought about them. "Well, I guess we'll just have milk again."

16

His mother shook her head. "Milk is a good food, but it is not enough."

"How can we get more food?" Jack asked.

His mom said softly, "I can think of only one way."

Jack blinked. "What way is that?"

His mother said, "You will have to get a rope."

"I know where to find a rope," Jack said. He ran outside to his yard and fetched the rope. He picked it up in his mouth and hurried back to his mother. *"Here's a wope,"* he said. It was hard to talk with his mouth full! *"So far, so goo'!"*

"I can hardly understand what you are saying. Tie the rope around Blossom's neck."

"I can tie a goo' knot," Jack said. *"'At's easy!"*

"Now you will have to take Blossom into town."

Jack dropped the rope. "I know every step of the way," he said.

"You will have to sell Blossom and buy some food with the money you get."

Jack couldn't believe his ears. "Sell Blossom?" he asked, his heart sinking. "To someone else?"

"That's all we can do," Jack's mother said. "She's all we have. Use the money from selling her to buy us some food."

Jack's heart pounded. What would happen when that food was gone? Then he and his mother would have nothing at all! They might starve to death!

"I can't sell Blossom," Jack said sadly. His ears drooped. His tail drooped. "She's like a friend!" He tried to think of another reason. He said, "She's teaching me to moo!"

"We have to do it, Jack," his mother said.

Jack tried to think of some other answer. He didn't want to sell Blossom. Finally, he tied the rope around Blossom's neck.

"I'm sorry," Jack told the cow. "But you are all we have, and we need food. I will try to sell you to someone who will be kind to you."

"Moo," Blossom said, as if she understood Jack's problem.

Jack left the yard and walked slowly toward town. He held the rope in his teeth. Blossom walked slowly behind him. They came to a bridge over a river.

Sitting beside the bridge was a strange little man. He wore a shirt that was yellow, red, blue, green, and purple. His pants were purple, green, blue, red, and yellow. His hat was as tall as he was. He stood up as Jack and Blossom came close to the bridge.

"It is about time you got here!" the strange little man said.

Jack took the rope out of his mouth. "Who are you?" he asked.

"I'm a man who is looking for a good cow," he said. "Yours seems to be a fine one. I want to buy her."

Jack sighed. "Will you be kind to her?" he asked.

"Of course I will," the man said. "I will

give the cow her very own room to sleep in. I will serve her food on a silver plate. I will sing to her as I milk her."

"All right," Jack said. He wagged his tail politely. "How much money will you give me for her?"

"I don't have any money," the odd man said. "But I will trade you something for your cow. What would you like?"

"My mother and I need food," Jack said.

The man thought and thought. Then he sat down and smiled. "I will trade you a nice ham for the cow," he said.

Jack's mouth watered. But he was too smart to be fooled. "Just one ham?"

"It's a big ham," the man answered.

Jack said, "No, thank you. After my mother and I ate the ham, we would be worse off than we are now."

The man frowned and walked in a circle. Then he stopped. He said, "I will give you ten pounds of carrots, ten pounds of potatoes, and ten pounds of spinach for your cow."

Jack was smart enough to know he could make a better deal. He made a face. "Yuck! I hate spinach!"

The man folded his arms. He tapped his foot on the ground. "You are making this hard," he said. Then he smiled again. "I know! I will give you three beans for your cow!"

Jack shook his head so hard that his ears flapped. "Did I hear you right? Did you say *three* beans?" He thought to himself, *This has got to be a trick!* He told the man, "If I wouldn't take a ham, or carrots, potatoes, and—yuck!—spinach, why should I take three beans?"

The man winked. He whispered, "These

beans are worth more than food or money. You see, these are *magic* beans! If you plant these beans when the moon is full, they will grow into a special beanstalk. That beanstalk will lead you to happiness." He took a small leather pouch from inside his shirt. "Happiness can be yours, just for selling your cow!"

Jack felt excited. But he was smart enough to think things through. "When will the moon be full?" he asked. "My mom and I can't wait long, because we haven't any food. That's why I have to sell our cow."

"You're in luck," said the man. "The moon will be full tonight! Plant the beans and then stand back!"

"Stand back?" asked Jack.

"Yes, just stand back. That's all I can say!" answered the man. "So, do we have a deal?"

Jack wanted his mother to be happy. He thought about the beans. He thought about what the man had said. Even if he sold Blossom for enough money to buy a lot of food, the food would be gone before long. Then he and his mother would go hungry again.

"All right," Jack told the man. "I'll take the magic beans! Here's our cow. Her name is Blossom. She likes her grass very green."

The man patted Blossom's neck. "She's a fine cow," he said. "She'll like being my cow, and I'll be kind to her. Here are your beans."

The man held out the little pouch. Jack took it carefully in his teeth. "*Hank you,*" he said.

"You are welcome," the man told him. "Remember, plant them tonight, and then stand back. Tomorrow you'll have a wonderful surprise!"

The man led Blossom across the bridge. Jack felt lonely as he watched his faithful cow walk away. He felt the same kind of ache in his heart that he got whenever he thought about his father.

Then Jack turned and ran all the way back home. He cheered up as he went. Now

Jack couldn't wait to tell his mother what a great deal he had made. He knew she would be surprised at first. Maybe she would even be upset. Then she would be happy when he explained that the beans were magical!

They must be very magical, Jack thought. Ordinary beans couldn't make people happy.

Chapter Three

Can You Hear the Beanstalk?

Jack ran home as fast as his paws could carry him. He gripped the bag of beans tightly in his teeth. He was glad he had been clever. An ordinary person might have been tricked in a trade like the one he had made.

He laughed to himself. It would have been silly to trade Blossom for just one meal, or even for enough food for a week. Magic beans would be better.

Jack wondered what the magic would do. Maybe it would grant him three wishes. Jack already knew what he would wish for. He would wish for food, and then for more food! After that, he would wish for even more food.

Maybe the magic beans would turn into a beanstalk that grew all kinds of tasty food. Jack imagined steaks and pork chops growing on a beanstalk. Beside them grew ripe bananas and juicy watermelons. Near them grew turkeys and sweet corn. That would be a very tasty kind of magic, indeed!

As Jack ran, he thought of other kinds of magic. Each kind he thought about seemed better than the one before. He could not wait to find out what the three beans really would do.

He arrived at his house. Jack jumped up and scratched at the door. He continued to hold the bag of beans tightly in his teeth.

Jack's mother came to the door and opened it. "Are you back so soon?" she asked as Jack walked inside.

Jack tried to talk. It was hard to speak when he was holding that bag of beans in his teeth. *"Yeth, Mother,"* he said. *"I did vhat you tol' me to do. I thold our cow."*

"You did what?" his mother asked.

"I thold our cow! I thold Blothom," he said. *"Take thith bag and you'll thee."*

"I can't understand you," she said.

Jack dropped the bag from his mouth and said, "I said I sold our cow! I sold Blossom! Look in the bag and see what I got for her!"

His mother seemed surprised. She opened the bag. She looked inside. Her eyes grew very wide. "Jack," she said, "what are these?"

"They're magic beans!" Jack told his mom proudly.

The woman shook the beans out into her hand. One was red and shiny. One was blue and fuzzy. The third one was white and small. "These aren't magical!" Jack's mother said. "These are just plain beans that someone has painted!"

"No, Mom! The man who gave them to me told me they were magical," said Jack. "He told me to plant them tonight. They are going to grow into a magic beanstalk. Then we will have all the food we will ever need."

Jack's mother looked at him. "You traded our cow for magic beans?" she asked.

"Yes!" Jack said, wagging his tail happily. "Just plant these and then stand back!"

"Magic beans," his mother said. She was still looking at him.

"That's right!" Jack said. "We just have to plant these beans. Then stand back!"

"Wait," his mother said, rubbing her eyes. "Are you saying that you traded Blossom, our cow, for three beans? Blossom, who has been faithfully giving us milk and cheese for years. For three beans?"

Jack stopped wagging his tail. "Funny . . . when you say it like that, it sounds like a bad deal," Jack said.

His mother looked sad. She shook her head. "Oh, Jack, how could you have done such a thing?" she asked. "That cow was all we had in the whole world. Now all we have are these three beans."

"*Magic* beans," said Jack. "Mom, you keep leaving that part out."

"Well, what are these beans supposed to do?" Jack's mother asked.

Jack thought for a moment. "Well . . . they do . . . magic stuff!"

His mother shook her head again. "Jack, these are not magic beans. There are no such things as magic beans."

Jack shook his head. "Of course they are magical! Why would the man tell me they were if it wasn't true?"

"Jack, there are no such things as magic beans!" his mother said again. Her face was turning red.

Was she right? Had the strange man cheated Jack out of a perfectly good cow?

"The man told me they were magical," Jack said. He felt so bad that he covered his eyes with his paw. "Did I do something wrong?"

"Yes!" his mother said. "You traded our cow for three tiny beans!"

The kitchen window was open. Jack's mother looked at the beans sadly, and then tossed them out the window.

Jack blinked at her. "We could at least have eaten them," he said.

"No," his mother told him. "Three beans are not enough to cook. I will have to cook something else."

But they didn't have very much else. Jack went outside to their tiny garden and dug with his front paws. He found one little turnip. He brought it in to his mother.

She said, "This will have to do." She made turnip soup. It was very watery.

Jack thought the soup tasted terrible. He didn't complain, though, because he felt bad about the beans. That night he went to bed still feeling hungry.

Poor Jack lay in bed staring out the window. The night was dark. Then he saw a silver

light. It was the moon. He remembered what the strange little man had told him.

Jack wondered if he could find the beans. He slipped out of his bed. He went outside into the yard. He sniffed around in the grass outside the kitchen window.

He found the red bean and picked it up in his mouth. He moved it to a corner of the yard and dropped it. Then he sniffed again until he found the other two beans. He took both of them to the same corner.

Jack was so hungry that his tummy rumbled and growled. "This had better work," he said.

With his front paws, he dug a hole in the soft earth. Then he picked up the beans in his mouth. One by one, he dropped them into the hole he had made. Then he carefully covered them with dirt.

He stood back.

He waited.

Nothing happened.

After a long time, Jack went back inside.

His head drooped. His tail drooped. He felt awful. *I thought I was so smart*, he told himself. *But that man tricked me.*

When Jack was sure that nothing was going to happen, he got back into bed. Jack wanted to stay awake. Maybe the magic would take a little time to work. He was so tired. At last, his eyes closed and he fell asleep. . . .

That was when the magic started. Out in the yard the little hill of earth over the beans began to shiver. It began to shake. A tiny green shoot peeped out. The moonlight shone on it. It opened one leaf—*pop!* Then out came another, and another, and another. *Pop! Pop! Pop! Popopopop!*

Then that one little shoot began to grow!

Wow! What a great story! I can't believe Jack is sleeping through this part. But I know how he feels. It's getting close to my own nap time. And growing puppies need their rest. I just can't sleep now. I have to  think of a way to get my ball back. If I could just keep my . . . eyes . . . open . . . ZZZZZZzzzzzzzz.

Chapter Four

Wishbone and
the Giant

All Friday night Wishbone felt unhappy. He wanted his toy back! But no one would listen to him. The next morning was Saturday.

After breakfast, Joe asked his mother, "Can I take Wishbone to Jackson Park? David and I are going to play catch. Maybe Wishbone would like to play, too."

Ellen said, "Well, if you will promise to keep an eye on Wishbone, I think that would be all right. You and David be careful when you cross the streets. And be back home in time for lunch!"

Joe got Wishbone's leash. Wishbone knew what that meant, and he began to jump for joy! "Wait a minute, Joe! If we're going out to play, I want to get my—"

Then Wishbone remembered. His toy was at school, and he was too young to go to school by himself to get it. He sighed. Joe clipped his leash to his collar, and the two went out.

The day was bright and warm, but that didn't cheer Wishbone up. David Barnes came out of his house next door. He carried a soft-ball and a glove. "Hi, Joe!" he called. "Let's go and play ball!"

The boys walked to the park. Wishbone usually led the way when he and Joe were walking. The puppy liked to pull the leash tightly and run ahead, sniffing at everything. Today, though, he just walked beside Joe.

They passed a street, and from it came a familiar smell. Wishbone's ears perked up. His nose twitched. "Joe! I smell your school! It's just down that street! Could we go there and get my ball back?"

Joe tugged on the leash. "Come on, boy," he said. "Come on! Let's go!"

Wishbone kept looking back. "But, my ball! It's all alone in that great big place! Who knows what might happen to it? It's time to listen to the puppy!"

Joe didn't seem to hear. He and David just kept walking. Soon Wishbone, Joe, and David came to Jackson Park. There Joe took Wishbone's leash off. Joe and David played catch for a few minutes.

Then Wishbone smelled someone coming. He had been lying down in the warm grass. He jumped to his feet. "Sam's here! Here she comes!"

"Hi!" Sam called. She was wearing a baseball cap, and she was carrying a bat. "I'm glad you're here playing. Want to hit some flies and grounders?"

"Cool!" Joe said.

"Sure," David added with a laugh.

Wishbone sat and watched. Sam was real good with a bat. She could pop a fly ball way up into the blue sky, or send a line drive flying straight as an arrow. Then, with a sharp *crack!*, she could smack a ground ball and send it skimming over the grass. The boys took turns catching the softball and tossing it back to her. Sam continued hitting the ball.

Wishbone put his head down on his paws. He thought, *That looks like fun. I'd like to chase a ball, too. But I'd like to chase* my *ball. This one does not taste right.*

For a few more minutes he watched Sam hit the softball. Then Wishbone noticed that Joe was laughing and talking to Sam. He wasn't looking at Wishbone.

Wishbone remembered how close the school had smelled. It would take him just a few minutes to run there and come back. He wasn't supposed to go places without Joe—but then, his ball was not supposed to be at the school, either.

Wishbone felt a little nervous. He was just a puppy, and the school was a very big place. But he just *had* to have his soccer ball!

Wishbone stood up. Maybe he could dash over to the school, run inside, and get his ball. Maybe Joe wouldn't even notice he was gone!

The puppy slowly walked away from the game. He tiptoed quietly until he had passed some trees. Then he looked around. He could not see Joe, so he knew Joe couldn't see him.

Wishbone ran! He raced with his ears flapping in the wind and his nails clicking on the sidewalk. Before long he came to the street that he had smelled earlier. He turned and ran that way until he saw the school straight ahead.

Wishbone's tongue was hanging out. "Yes! Now all I have to do is get inside, grab my ball, and Joe will never know I was gone!"

Wishbone trotted up to the door. It was closed. He scratched at it and waited patiently. No one came to open it.

Wishbone scratched again. "Isn't anyone here? This place was full yesterday! Come on, people, let the cute puppy inside!"

Still no one came. Wishbone sighed. He turned to go back to the park. He hoped he wouldn't get in trouble for running away. If only Joe would listen to the puppy—

Suddenly, Wishbone heard a click, like a door opening! It came from the side of the school building! He dashed around the corner and skidded to a stop.

The biggest man Wishbone had ever seen came out a side door. He wore work gloves. He carried a huge plastic trash bag.

Through the open door Wishbone could see two other big plastic bags. *Whoa!* thought Wishbone. *A giant! With giant garbage!* The man was really big. Wishbone was afraid to walk up to him and wag his tail.

The man propped the door open. Wishbone hid under a bush and watched him. The big man picked up the trash bag and carried it to a big garbage can. He put the bag inside the can and then came back. He didn't notice that he was being spied on by a Jack Russell terrier.

"That's one down," the man said. Then he picked up the second trash bag and headed for the garbage can.

Wishbone swallowed hard. That was one *big* man!

But then Wishbone remembered the story of "Jack and the Beanstalk." *Jack was brave*, he thought. *He ran into a very big man, too. In fact,*

Jack ran into a giant! But he went marching right into the giant's castle because he was brave. . . . Well, I'm brave, too!

Wishbone peeked out from the bush. The man was putting another trash bag inside the garbage can. Wishbone ran for the door.

"Look out! Brave dog coming through!" In a flash, he darted right into the school building!

Wishbone looked back over his shoulder as he dashed down the hall. Had he made it inside without being seen? Or was the big man chasing him?

Was he safe, or in deep, deep trouble?

Jack is about to face a big, scary place himself. Let's see how he does there.

Chapter Five

Crowds of Clouds

That morning Jack woke up with a start. He heard his mother yelling!

"What? What is it?" Jack cried. He jumped out of bed and dressed quickly.

"Look at that!" shouted his mother. "It's going to fall on the house!"

Jack ran to the open doorway, where his mother stood. He looked past her and saw something that looked like a giant green tree with huge leaves. It towered up, up, up into the sky. Jack could not even see its top.

"Wow!" he said. "It's a giant beanstalk! I wonder what's at the top."

"Who could climb it to find out?" his mother asked.

"Me!" said Jack. "I remember the strange little man told me that the beans would lead me to happiness. All I have to do is follow the beanstalk now."

"Be careful, Jack," his mother said.

Jack ran to the beanstalk. He took one step onto a leaf. It supported his weight. Using his paws and teeth, he started to climb, one leaf at a time. Luckily, the beanstalk was really *three* beanstalks twisted around and around one another. It was like climbing a big spiral staircase.

"Hey, Mom, I'll come back as soon as I see what's at the top!" Jack yelled down. He climbed up and up, higher and higher.

Hours passed.

I wonder how high I am, Jack thought.

He looked down and saw the Earth far below. Everything looked like it did on a map. He saw rivers gleaming, mountains casting

long shadows, and farm fields like checker-boards of yellow and green. Jack felt the fur on his neck stand up. He swallowed hard.

"I'm high up. Very high up!"

Jack didn't look down again. At last he climbed up right through the highest clouds in the sky. He looked around in surprise.

"It looks like a country!" Jack said. The clouds rolled away in all directions like white hills. White trees grew on them, and white birds flew in the air. He saw something a long way off that looked like a big purple mountain.

Then Jack took a closer look and realized that it wasn't a mountain, but a castle—a *huge* castle. Jack took several steps toward it, and then he looked down. He was standing on the clouds, and they were just as hard as the ground.

"What is this place?" he asked.

"This is the Country of the Clouds," said a voice behind him.

Jack yipped in surprise and spun around.

A strange-looking woman floated in the air
behind him. She was gray-haired and plump.
She wore a pink, glittery gown and a pointy
hat. Strangest of all, she had two huge butterfly
wings of pink, blue, and black.

"Who are you?" Jack asked.

"I'm your Good Fairy," she said.

"You are my Good Fairy?" Jack asked. "I
didn't know I had a Good Fairy."

The fairy flapped her wings. "Listen

carefully, for you haven't much time. Do you see that castle over there?"

Jack shook his head. "Wait a minute. Does everyone have a Good Fairy?"

"There is no time for questions," the fairy said. "Do you see that castle over there?"

Jack looked over his shoulder. "Yes," Jack said. "It's gigantic."

"That's because it is a giant's castle," the fairy said. "In fact, it belongs to the giant who stepped on your father."

Jack growled. "I miss my dad," he said sadly.

The fairy looked kindly at Jack. "I know you do. He was a very good man."

"Wait a minute. Were you my dad's Good Fairy?" Jack asked.

"Yes," the fairy answered.

Jack said in surprise, "Then where were you when the giant was stepping on him and stealing his treasures?"

The fairy flapped her butterfly wings quickly. "There is *really* no more time for questions. Your life is in danger. The giant is cruel, and the people here in the Country of the Clouds are afraid of him. They need a hero to teach the giant a lesson. Do you know about your father's treasures?"

Jack said, "You mean the goose that lays golden eggs, the harp that plays itself, and the magic axe that chops wood by itself?"

"Yes!" said the fairy. "Are you brave enough to try to get them back?"

Jack almost pawed the earth . . . or he almost pawed the clouds. "Yes! That's what my father would have done," he said.

"Good," said the fairy. "Hurry to the castle and look for the treasures. Right now the giant is away, so this is your chance. Oh, here's something to put them in."

The fairy reached into a deep pocket in her gown. She fluttered close and handed Jack a small brown cloth bag.

Jack took it in surprise. "They must be very small treasures," he said.

The fairy laughed. "The bag is magic, too.

Do not worry. They will all fit. Now, run! Run!"

So Jack ran. He ran down a winding cloud path. It led over cloud bridges, up cloud hills, and through cloud woods. Cloud bugs buzzed by, cloud birds chirped overhead, and cloud flowers waved in the breeze.

No wonder they call this the Country of the Clouds, Jack thought. *Clouds to the left of me! Clouds to the right of me!*

Jack looked down. *I just hope these nice, solid clouds stay under my feet. It's a long way down if I fall through.*

After a long time Jack came right up to the castle. It was as big as a mountain. The front step was high over his head. Jack dug in all his paws. He counted, "One, two, three—go!" Then he made a mighty leap.

Jack barely made it to the step. The giant front door was closed. That was okay, though, because there was a space underneath it that was just wide enough for him to slip through.

Once he got inside the castle, Jack looked around. He couldn't believe what he saw. A giant hat stand that looked like a tree rose beside the door.

Deeper inside, Jack saw a table with one huge chair. A stool was beside it. The chair was twice the size of a big bed, and it was five times as high as a normal chair.

Jack began to shake a little. "This makes me feel really, really small!"

The moment he said that, Jack heard a loud *honk!* The sound seemed to come from up on the table.

Hmm . . . Jack thought. *What goes "honk"? A horn! Or a clown's nose! Or—don't tell me—a goose!*

One of his father's treasures was a goose that laid golden eggs. Jack had to see what was up on that table. He looked at the stool, then at the huge chair. He took a long run. He leaped. He landed on the stool! He jumped from the stool up to the chair. Then he jumped from the chair up onto the table!

There, in a golden cage, he saw a white goose. The goose looked at him with sad eyes. "Honk," she said.

Jack felt a lump in his throat. "You used to belong to my dad," he said softly. "I wonder what Dad would do if he were here."

"Honk," said the goose.

Jack made up his mind. "If by 'Honk' you mean to say, 'Your dad would save me from the giant,' I think you're right. And that's just what I'll do, too!"

Jack had tucked the magic bag into his shirt. He was just pulling it out when he heard a sound. Someone stood behind him.

Was it the giant?

Wow! Jack is finding out that exploring strange places can be exciting. And scary, too! Of course, real life can also be scary. I am learning that myself, inside Joe's school, as I look for my soccer ball. . . .

Chapter Six

Inside, but Nowhere to Hide!

Back inside Oakdale Elementary School, Wishbone was having trouble. The school was so big! How could he find Miss Basso's classroom?

Wishbone put his nose to the floor and sniffed. He walked through the hallways until he could smell a familiar scent. That was Joe!

Wishbone was finding out that people and animals left scent trails—trails that he could follow! He followed Joe's trail eagerly until he found . . . the boys' rest room.

Okay, okay, I remember, he thought. *I just have to go the other way*. With his nose to the

57

floor, Wishbone followed the scent backward. Finally, he found Miss Basso's classroom, but the door was closed.

For a little while, Wishbone sat down in the hall and just stared up at the doorknob. He wondered why people didn't put them low enough for a dog to reach.

Then Wishbone heard the big man coming. He remembered his scent. The man's heavy footsteps echoed loudly in the empty halls, and he was humming.

Wishbone looked around wildly for a place to hide. He found a spot behind a water fountain. He huddled there, making himself as small as he could.

From his hiding spot, Wishbone watched the man as he came pounding down the hall, step by step. He pushed a rolling trash can and carried a big broom. The man stopped at the first classroom door and unlocked it. He opened it and went inside. Wishbone's sharp ears heard the sound of sweeping.

Wishbone crept out from his hiding place. He walked carefully to the doorway, almost on tiptoes. He peeked into the room just in time to see the big man empty a dustpan into his rolling trash can.

"That's one down," the man said, and he started to hum again.

The trash can rolled toward Wishbone. Where could he hide? He thought fast. As the can rolled into the hall, Wishbone ducked behind it. He walked along just in front of the can, keeping himself low. Maybe the man wouldn't see him!

The can stopped rolling. As the man walked around it one way, Wishbone walked around it the opposite way. He heard the man unlock another classroom door. Wishbone noticed that the man had not closed the first door down the hall.

Great! thought Wishbone. *All I have to do is wait until he opens the door of Miss Basso's classroom. He'll sweep the room and leave. Then I can get inside. . . .*

He couldn't hide behind the rolling trash can for long. The man would be sure to spot him sooner or later.

Oh, no! Wishbone thought. *That just isn't fair! I'm so close to my soccer ball!* He needed another place to hide—and quickly! Where could he hide next?

Then the puppy got a wonderful idea. As the man pulled the trash can inside the second classroom, Wishbone ran down the hall. With a clatter of nails on the hard floor, he dived into the open classroom! It was not Miss Basso's classroom. But he would wait there until it was safe to get his ball.

At least that was his plan. Wishbone dashed through the opened doorway just in time to hear the man yell, "What was that? Who's there?"

Wishbone looked around the classroom for a place to hide. He could hear the man's heavy footsteps coming. He darted into a space between two bookshelves.

Lying there, Wishbone saw the man come through the opened doorway. He heard the man say, "I know I heard something!" He watched the man's big shoes coming closer and closer to the spot where he was hiding.

Busted! The huge man is on to me. Maybe Jack is having better luck finding his treasures.

Chapter Seven

GIANT Problems!

Jack stood on the giant's table and heard a sound behind him.

"A mouse! There's a mouse on the table! Help!" someone cried.

Jack spun around, surprised to hear a girl's voice. "I'm not a mouse!" he yelled. "I'm Jack! I'm Jack!"

Standing on the table across from him was a girl. She wasn't a giant. She was normal-sized. She was pretty and dark-haired. She had her hands pressed to her mouth in fear. "It's just been so long since I have seen someone who isn't a giant."

"Have you ever seen a mouse as big as I am?" Jack asked.

"Here, they're all as big as you are," the girl told him. "They're giant mice."

"Well, this is a giant's castle, I guess." Jack quickly explained who he was and what he wanted to do. "This was my father's goose," he told the girl. "The giant stole it, along with my father's magic harp and magic axe. I just want to get them all back."

"I'd love to see you do it," the girl said. "The giant isn't very nice. He came down to Earth and stole me. Now he makes me do all the housekeeping here at his castle. Work, work, work—that's all I ever do!"

"It must be hard," Jack said. "This is a big place to keep clean."

"Hard!" the girl said. "How would you like to wash a plate as big as a wading pool? How would you like to chase dust bunnies that are bigger than you are? I've been here so long. I dream of a prince who will come and rescue me. A tall, handsome prince. A prince who would want to marry me—"

Jack looked around. "I'm not a prince, but I will be happy to rescue you."

"You will?" the girl asked.

"If you'll help me," Jack said, "I'll take you with me when I leave, and you'll be free. But we've just met. It's too early to think about marriage!"

"All right. Then I will settle for being

rescued. And I'll help you!" the girl promised. "My name is Daisy."

"All right, Daisy," Jack said, glad that he had a friend in this dangerous place. "Hold this bag for me. I'm going to put the goose in it!"

Jack picked up the golden cage. He stuffed a corner of the cage into the bag. He dragged it over to Daisy.

"She'll never fit!" Daisy said, as she took hold of the bag.

The cage shrank as it slipped into the bag. Then the goose's feet shrank! The goose looked at the bag in alarm. In a loud voice, she said, "**Honk!Honk!**Honk!" Even her honking sound shrank as she slid inside the bag!

"There!" Jack said. "This is truly a magic bag! It will hold anything. Now, for the next two treasures. Do you know where the harp and the axe are?"

"The harp is in the music room," Daisy

said. "That's only about half a mile away. Come with me!"

They jumped from the table to the chair, from the chair to the stool, and from the stool to the floor. Jack followed Daisy down a long, long hallway. Soon he heard music. A harp was playing a soft, sad song.

Daisy and Jack pushed open a huge door. Luckily, it had to open only a crack for them to slip inside. Jack saw the harp in a corner.

"Harp," he said, "I'm Jack Terrier. I'm here to rescue you!"

The harp began to play a happy tune.

"Into the bag," Jack said. Just like the goose and its cage, the harp shrank as Jack slipped it right into the bag. The bag didn't seem to get any bigger or heavier.

"Now for the axe!" Jack said.

"The axe is on the back step, beside the back door," Daisy said. "Hurry! It's almost time for the giant to come home!"

They ran all the way. Jack found the axe and

slid it into the magic bag with the goose and the harp. "Now, let's get out of here!" he said.

They hurried through the back door. They ran down the long, long hallway. They came closer and closer to the front door.

And then the front door suddenly opened in front of them.

Someone stood in the doorway. Someone who was very, very big.

Jack skidded to a stop. "Don't tell me . . ." Jack said.

Daisy ran into him from behind. "It's the giant!" she whispered.

"I told you *not* to tell me that," Jack said quietly.

Then, in a voice like a clap of thunder, the giant boomed, "Fee! Fi! Fo! Fum! I smell the blood of an Englishman!"

"What does 'Fee! Fi! Fo! Fum!' mean?" Jack asked.

"I don't know. He always says that when he's hungry," Daisy said.

"So what does he like to eat?" Jack asked. "Maybe we can get him some food to calm him down."

The giant stomped his way closer. His terrible voice thundered again. "Be he alive or be he dead, I will grind his bones to make my bread!"

"On second thought, I'm not ready to be someone's dinner roll," Jack whispered. "We have to get out of here—fast!"

The giant had not seen them yet. Jack knew they couldn't hide from someone that big—not for long. But he was smart enough to think of a plan.

He grabbed the bag in his teeth and said, *"Daisy, whump into the bag!"*

"What?" she said.

"Whump into the bag!" Jack said.

"Oh. '*Jump* into the bag.' But there's not enough room!" she whispered.

"Trust me!" Jack whispered back as he set the bag down.

The floor shook as the giant walked into

the castle. He roared, "Fee! Fi! Fo! Fum! I hear the voice of an Englishman!"

Daisy jumped into the bag without another word. The harp started to play.

"This would be a good time for the harp to stop playing," Jack said, trying to hide under a stool.

The harp played a little louder.

"Helllooo! I said you can stop playing now," Jack whispered.

The giant snatched up the stool. He glared down at Jack.

"Too late," Jack said. He grabbed the bag and ran for his life!

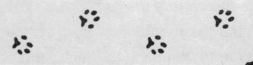

Jack is in trouble, all right! But at least he had found his treasures before he got into trouble.

Back in Oakdale, I'm having problems of my own—and I still have not found my ball!

Chapter Eight

A Trapped Terrier

Wishbone knew he had to do what Jack did. He ran from his hiding place. He headed for the door!

"There you are!" boomed the custodian, stepping in front of him. "Come here, you!"

Wishbone turned. He crawled under a row of desks in the classroom. "I'm . . . uh . . . just a piece of chalk! Rolling along. No?"

The man was picking up the desks one by one!

The puppy moved even faster. The man continued to look for him. There was only one way out—

Wishbone ran between the man's legs!

"Stop! Stop, you!" said the custodian.

The teacher's desk! It had to be too big for the man to lift! Wishbone dived under the chair and slid beneath the desk. It was like a dark cave underneath the desk. He scrunched into a corner. He hoped the man hadn't seen where he had gone—

"Oh, no! A hand!" Wishbone said. It was reaching down for him. . . .

The man took Wishbone out. "Where did *you* come from?" the custodian asked.

Wishbone squirmed. "Well . . . I live in a nice house, with my best friend, Joe, and—"

"Wishbone," the custodian said in a booming voice.

Wishbone blinked. "Huh? How do you know my name?" Then Wishbone remembered that his name was right on his dog tag.

"And here's the phone number of your owner," the man said as he examined Wishbone's dog tag. "I think I'd better make a call."

Oh, great, Wishbone thought. That meant Joe and Ellen would find out about all the trouble he was in.

The custodian held on to Wishbone and didn't let him have a chance to wiggle free. He took the puppy to an office. The custodian closed the door before he put Wishbone down. Wishbone sat on a round rug and looked up at the man.

"Now, wait a minute, buddy. I'm not just a

Jack Russell terrier. I'm an American! I have rights! It is illegal to hold me captive. Uh . . . you're not buying any of this, are you? Okay, how about this?" Wishbone made his eyes big and round. "Oh, please let me go. Please, please, please, please?"

"Now, don't look at me like that," the man said. "A little guy like you shouldn't be out all alone. My name is Matt, by the way." Matt picked up the phone and dialed a number. After a moment, Wishbone heard him say, "Hello? Is this the person who owns a puppy named Wishbone?"

Wishbone closed his eyes. "A puppy who hardly ever gets into trouble! Tell them that! A puppy who's usually a good puppy!"

Matt laughed. "He's fine, Mrs. Talbot. This is Matt Stromberg, the custodian at Oakdale Elementary. Somehow, this little guy got into the school. . . . Oh, sure, I'll wait for you and Joe. He's no trouble. He's a handsome little guy."

Matt hung up the phone.

"Well, Wishbone," Matt said, "you're in luck. Joe and his mom were very worried about you. They'll be right over to pick you up. I think you got Joe in trouble, though."

Wishbone lay down. "I sure am in trouble. I— What? How did I get Joe in trouble? I didn't mean to do that!"

"Joe was supposed to watch you," Matt went on. "I think his mom may be a bit upset with him because you ran away."

Wishbone closed his eyes. This was getting worse and worse! How could he ever explain? Especially when no one listened to the puppy!

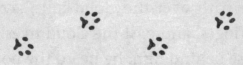

Things still don't look good in Oakdale! And, just like me, Jack finds himself being chased by a very large man—a very large man with a big appetite! I sure hope that Jack has better luck than I've had.

Chapter Nine

It's Raining Giants!

Jack ran right between the giant's huge feet! His nails clattered on the floor. The giant had left the castle's front door open! Jack leaped off the front step! He raced down the winding path over the cloud hills, across the cloud bridges, and past the cloud trees!

Close behind him, he heard the pounding footsteps of the giant! They made the path quake! They sounded like a huge elephant dribbling a couple of basketballs!

The giant roared, "Fee! Fi! Fo! Fum! I'm going to catch you! Here I come!"

Ahead of him, Jack saw his Good Fairy.

She fluttered in the air around and around the beanstalk. "Hurry!" she yelled. "He is right behind you!"

Jack looked back for a moment. Then he turned to face the fairy. "Nice to see you. But I could have used a little help inside the castle, you know."

"Climb down the beanstalk, and then you'll know what to do! Good luck!" the fairy said.

"What do you mean, I'll know what to do?" Jack asked. "Why don't you just tell me?"

"You must hurry. There is no time for questions," the fairy said.

Jack started to make his way down the beanstalk. *She never has time for questions. I wonder if the Good Fairies have a complaint department.* He raced down the winding spiral. The whole beanstalk shook as the giant climbed on right above him.

"Whoa!" Jack muttered to himself, keeping a tight grip on the magic bag. "Don't look up! Don't look up!"

Jack kept his head down and saw the ground far below.

"Whoa!" he said. He felt dizzy. "I'm still so high up! Don't look down! Don't look down!"

He heard the giant's rumbling voice right above him.

They both slid down the beanstalk, faster and faster.

Jack kept ahead of the giant. He finally dared to look down. Right below him, he saw the little house where he lived with his mother! And there she stood!

Jack scrambled down a few more feet. Then he jumped!

"Jack!" his mother cried as he landed on the ground. "Where in the world have you been? And what's in that bag? More beans?"

"No, Mother," Jack said, shaking the bag.

Daisy flew out and landed on the grass with a thump. She stood up. "Oh, we're back on Earth!" she exclaimed. "Hello, I'm Daisy."

Jack shook the bag again. The goose flew out, still in its cage.

Once again, Jack shook the bag. The harp fell out. It was *still* playing. Everything coming out of the bag was returning to its normal size.

Jack shook the bag once more. The magic axe flew out at last! And just in time! The shadow of the giant was blocking out the sun!

"Axe, axe, work for me!" Jack yelled, trying to use words that would make the axe chop. "Chop, chop, chop, chop down that . . . uh . . . beanstalk."

"Oh!" cried Jack's mother. She had finally seen the giant.

"Jack, nothing's happening," said Daisy. "What's wrong?"

"I don't know! I *am* trying!" Jack said. "Maybe the words have to rhyme!" He thought hard and then yelled, "Axe, axe, work or *walk!* Chop, chop, chop, chop down that *stalk!* Sometime today would be nice!"

The axe flew into the air! It began to chop

at the beanstalk! Bits of beanstalk flew everywhere! In a moment the beanstalk began to swing. It began to sway. It began to fall.

Then from far, far overhead, Jack, Daisy, and Jack's mother heard the giant yell:

"Oooohh Nooooooooo!"

BOOM!

For a long time Jack couldn't see anything because dust filled the air. Then it settled. Jack saw that the beanstalk had fallen, and the axe had chopped it up into beanstalk logs. The logs made a cozy green beanstalk-log cabin.

There was no sign of the giant. There was only a large hole in the ground, so deep that no one could see the bottom. The giant might have fallen all the way through the Earth. Or maybe he was stuck all the way down at the very bottom. No matter, he was gone for good!

Daisy said, "Thank you for saving me, Jack! You are so smart!"

Jack felt proud of himself. He trotted over to the new cabin and ran inside. There was a wonderful roomy kitchen, a big living room, and six or seven other rooms, too. Jack ran back out.

"Mom, this place is great!" he said with joy. "It has lots of bedrooms!

"Daisy," he said, looking at the pretty girl, "if you don't have any place to live, you can stay here with us. Think of it as a vacation from cleaning a giant castle."

Jack turned back to his mother. "Isn't this great! I got everything back from the giant! Here's the axe, there's the harp, and here's the goose that lays golden eggs." He opened the cage and the goose walked out, flapping her wings.

"Are you sure that's her?" asked Jack's mother. "I thought your father's goose was larger. That one looks like a plain old white goose."

"Well," Jack said, "if it isn't Dad's goose, you know lots of recipes for roast goose."

The goose looked alarmed. She sat down. In a second she laid a dozen golden eggs!

"I knew she could do it!" Jack said, laughing. "With that gold, we can buy all the food we want! And we've got a great, beanstalk-log cabin. And a big giant-shaped hole in the backyard. What more could we want?"

Jack's mother hugged him. "I'm so happy! We'll never be hungry again!"

Jack smiled so big that his tongue hung out.

"Oh, Jack," his mother said softly. "Your father would be so proud of you! You outsmarted the giant!"

"I may be small," Jack said, "but I'm very clever. And I can run like the wind!"

"All our troubles are over," his mother said.

"And now," said Jack, grinning, "I just want to live happily ever after! And maybe send out for some pizza!"

Things are looking up for Jack. Of course, I'm *still* in trouble back in Oakdale. And I *still* don't have my ball!

Chapter Ten

Wishbone's Last Chance

Wishbone wished that *he* could live happily ever after. When Ellen and Joe got to the school, Joe scooped Wishbone right up. "I was so worried!" he said. "Why did you run away?"

Wishbone squirmed. "Well . . . there's this ball, see—"

"Joe," Ellen said, "I hope you have learned that you have to watch out for Wishbone."

"I have, Mom," Joe told her. "I was playing with Sam and David, and I just forgot. I won't let it happen again."

"No harm done," Matt said. "I wonder why he came here to school, though."

Joe put Wishbone down and was about to clip his leash on. Wishbone saw the door was open. He ran through and headed for Miss Basso's classroom!

"Wishbone! No!" Joe yelled.

Wishbone ran straight to Miss Basso's classroom door and began to scratch at it. "Sorry, Joe! A puppy's got to do what a puppy's got to do!"

"I wonder what he wants," Matt said, as he and the others followed Wishbone. "Let's see." He opened the classroom door.

Wishbone ran inside. He raced over to a big bookcase in one corner. He lay on the floor and began to wiggle and squirm to get under the bookcase.

"What's he after?" Ellen asked.

"I don't know," Joe said.

Aha! Wishbone touched it with his nose! He wiggled a little more, opened his mouth, and felt his teeth close tightly on his favorite toy! He dragged it out from under the book-case. Wishbone saw Joe and set down his ball. "See? See? It was this! I had to get this!"

"His ball!" Joe said. "He must have left it here! That's why he came back!"

"Oh, Wishbone," Ellen said with a laugh. "I wish we'd known! We never would have left your favorite toy behind!"

Joe clipped Wishbone's leash to his collar. "Come on, buddy. I'll carry your ball until we get home," he said. "See, Mom? I'm not the only one who loses things!"

Wishbone trotted along happily beside Joe. "Lose it? I didn't lose it! I knew just where it was every minute! The problem was that I just couldn't put my paw on it!"

As usual, Ellen and Joe didn't seem to be listening. Wishbone sighed. He'd learned some things today. He'd learned that he could go out by himself and have adventures—even though that could get him in trouble. Most of all, he'd learned that even a giant-sized problem could be solved. Of course, to solve it, you might need to be as smart as Jack.

Or, Wishbone thought happily as they all got into the car, you might need to be as smart as a Jack Russell terrier!

About "Jack and the Beanstalk"

People all over the world tell stories about small, tricky, clever heroes. Native Americans tell about the Trickster, who can be anything from a raven to a coyote. Africans have Anansi the spider, who is very small but very tricky. Germans have Til Eulenspiegel, who causes a load of mischief wherever he goes. In England, though, Jack is the king of the small adventurers.

Jack fought giants, found treasures, and outsmarted bad guys. "Jack and the Beanstalk" is one of his most famous adventures. The tale goes back hundreds of years. In writing *Jack and the Beanstalk*, Brad Strickland and Thomas E. Fuller used two versions of the story: *The History of Mother Twaddle and the Marvelous Achievements of her Son Jack*, by an author who signed himself B.A.T.; and *The History of Mother Twaddle and the Marvellous*

Atchievements of her Son Jack, by H.A.C. The first was published in London in 1807, and the second one appeared in Philadelphia in 1809. Brad and Thomas thought that "Terrier" would be a better last name for Jack than "Twaddle"!

When some people left England and settled in colonies in America, they brought their stories along with them. Of course, Jack came, too. Today, in many parts of the country, people know "Jack Tales," which are American stories that use the same little, smart hero. It's nice to think that although he is small, Jack has traveled all around the world as the tricky, clever star of wonderful stories.

About Brad Strickland

Brad Strickland is a college teacher and writer who has written or cowritten more than thirty books. In the WISHBONE series, he wrote the first two books in The Adventures of Wishbone series, *Salty Dog* and *Be a Wolf!* Together with Thomas E. Fuller, he has written many WISHBONE Mysteries.

Brad was born in a little town called New Holland, Georgia. When he was young, he often heard his grown-up relatives telling funny or amazing stories. He thinks that this experience probably inspired him to want to be a writer.

He teaches English at Gainesville College. He is married, and his wife, Barbara, has co-written books with him. They like to travel, and they like pets. In fact, they have ferrets, cats, dogs, and an African chameleon. They have two children, Jonathan and Amy.

Jonathan has a Jack Russell terrier named Falstaff, who has just about as much energy as Wishbone, and he gets into almost as much trouble as Jack!

About Thomas E. Fuller

Thomas E. Fuller has been writing books and plays for children for more than twenty years. With his writing partner, Brad Strickland, he has written five WISHBONE Mysteries: *The Treasure of Skeleton Reef*, *Riddle of the Wayward Books*, *Drive-In of Doom*, *The Disappearing Dinosaurs*, and *Disoriented Express*.

When he isn't writing for WISHBONE, Thomas is the head writer for the Atlanta Radio Theatre Company, and playwright-in-residence for the Abracadabra Children's Theatre. He has published a number of short stories and poems, and his radio plays have been heard all across America—especially at Halloween.

Thomas and his artist wife, Berta, have four children: Edward, Anthony, John, and Christina. They share a very cluttered blue house in Duluth, Georgia, with a large collection of books and audiotapes, stacks of manuscripts and paintings, all the children in the neighborhood, two dogs—Cookie and Rags—and a gigantic twenty-pound orange cat called The General.